STUDY SKILLED...NOT!!!

Published by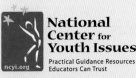

National Center for Youth Issues

Practical Guidance Resources
Educators Can Trust

www.ncyi.org

For Bubba,

Julia

Duplication and Copyright

No part of this publication may be reproduced, stored in a retrieval system or transmitted in any form by any means, electronic, mechanical, photocopy, recording or otherwise without prior written permission from the publisher except for all worksheets and activities which may be reproduced for a specific group or class. Reproduction for an entire school or school district is prohibited.

National Center for Youth Issues

Practical Guidance Resources
Educators Can Trust

ncyi.org

P.O. Box 22185
Chattanooga, TN 37422-2185
423.899.5714 • 866.318.6294
fax: 423.899.4547 • www.ncyi.org

ISBN: 978-1-937870-42-3
© 2016 National Center for Youth Issues, Chattanooga, TN
All rights reserved.
Written by: Julia Cook
Illustrations by: Michelle Hazelwood Hyde
Design by: Phillip W. Rodgers
Contributing Editor: Beth Spencer Rabon
Published by National Center for Youth Issues • Softcover
Printed at Starkey Printing, Chattanooga, Tennessee, U.S.A., December 2016

My name is Cletus.

Sometimes I have a hard time studying...especially at home.

I have to go to school every day for like 54 hours

and then I'm supposed to come home and study for 64 more hours at night!

I DON'T THINK SO!!!!!

If I studied everything I'm supposed to study every day and every night, I'd never have time to play!

Bocephus is my cousin. He lives down the street.

He's a **STUDY FREAK!!!**

Bocephus always says:

"You can't be too prepared when you're going to take a test.
That means you have to study a lot if you want to do your best.
And when it comes to studying, Cletus...
you're just not very good at it!"

Bocephus studies at home,
and he always studies at school.

He studies at the movies,
and even at the pool!

He makes all kinds of
flashcards
and practices
drill after drill.

My mom always tells me
that Bocephus is

STUDY-SKILLED!

But if he ever accidentally studies the wrong thing, it totally

STRESSES

him out.

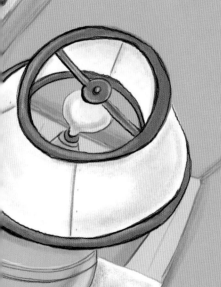

Last week, Bocephus started pre-studying for our science test on rocks and minerals. He had the whole chapter memorized. Then, our teacher decided to skip that chapter and do the one on the digestive system instead.

Bocephus just about lost it!

"I can't handle this, Mom! My life is just a mess!!!

I spent all my time on this chapter. She skipped it, and now I'm

"Chill out Bocephus...Don't stress out. All you do is study!

Why can't you be more relaxed like Cletus? Now that's how you should be!"

"But we have a test on Friday!!! And it's already Monday!!!
And I haven't even started studying for it!!!!"

"Why don't you try studying with Cletus?

Two heads are always better than one.

Besides, explaining something to another person is one of the best ways to find out what you really know (and/or don't know.)"

"Hi Cletus...Want to study the digestive system chapter with me?"

"Why?"

"Because we have a test on it this Friday!!!"

"But Bocephus...

it's only Monday!"

**"Cletus would just LOVE to study with you!!
Wouldn't you, Cletus...say YES!
You and Bocephus can study together!"**

"Well...OK...I guess."

So Bocephus and I headed to my room to start studying.

"I can't study in here, Cletus!
There's no place to set up my stuff!"

"What's all that junk anyway?
Isn't your textbook enough???"

"Cletus! These are my supplementary materials that will help me thoroughly understand the digestive system process!"

"What's to understand?

Food goes in, digestion takes place, and then other stuff comes out.

…how hard can it be?"

Just then, my mom came into my bedroom.

"Your study area is ready boys.
Come into the kitchen with me.

The dining room table is all cleared off,
and it's as quiet as can be!"

*"I don't think this is going to work out, Mom.
Bocephus doesn't study like me."*

"Well you don't study at all, Cletus!

That's why you have a  *!"*

**"Don't worry
about that boys.
Studying doesn't have
to be so tough.**

**As long as you do the
'AMAZING GREAT 8,'
it won't seem
near as rough."**

"What's the **AMAZING GREAT 8?**"

"Well, it just happens to be the most amazing study skill tips that have ever existed!!!"

"Pay attention, and take good notes.

Plan ahead for projects and tests.

Break the big stuff down into smaller chunks,

so it will fit inside your head!

**Ask for help
if you get stuck,**

**and organize
all of your stuff.**

**Always remember
to get enough sleep,**

**so your life doesn't
seem so rough.**

**Keep your focus
and stay on task.**

**So you won't waste
too much time.**

**Keep your
attitude positive,**

**and you'll end up
doing just fine!"**

"That's it? That's
all there is to it?"

"Yep!"

19

Bocephus and I talked it over, and we decided to give the AMAZING GREAT 8 a try.

My mom let us use the dining room table,
and we made a list of what we would need.

Textbooks, our folders, supplies, and that's it!
And Bocephus finally agreed.

Bocephus wrote out a great study plan,
so we could get everything done.

I drew pictures and glued them to flashcards,
to make things a little more fun.

We had a great time with our highlighters.
Coloring all of the important stuff.

Bocephus wanted to highlight everything...
"No Bocephus! That's enough!"

We really tried hard to listen in class,
so we could learn things the first time around.

I wrote down a lot more, and Bocephus wrote less,
but together, we got it all down.

We decided to go tech-free
when we studied.

No computers, games
or phones.

This kept our brains
from short-circuiting,

which happens a lot
when I'm home.

We broke the big stuff up into smaller parts,
so it would fit inside our heads.

We couldn't believe how much easier it was,
to remember what we had read.

We quizzed each other
every night.
We played study games
to make it more fun.

We only studied
40 minutes a day.

But WOW!

We got SO
much done!!!

When we got stuck on something, or didn't understand, we asked our teacher for help.

I just couldn't believe how easy it was and how great both of us felt.

The night before the digestive test,
we both got to bed by nine.

We made it to school today a little bit early,
so we would have plenty of time.

I was so excited to take that test!...
In fact, I could hardly wait!!!!

For the first time EVER I felt really prepared
thanks to doing the

AMAZING GREAT 8!

Bocephus aced the test...
of course.

And guess what???

I got a  **B** !!!!

There is more to digestion
than I had thought.

It's not as easy as

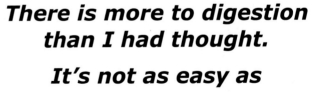

29

"Hi, Bocephus. What's up?"

"Want to study for
our Egypt test?
We only have 3 weeks!"

"Seriously????"

30

Teaching Children to be STUDY-SKILLED!

Having good study skills can make a huge difference when it comes to succeeding in both school and in life. However, good study skills are not innate…they must be taught, embraced and cultivated. Here are a few tips that may make that process easier.

1. Reinforce the purpose of having good study skills. Kids must "buy into" why having good study skills is beneficial, (i.e. you will have more free time, you will feel better about yourself when you do well…etc.)

2. Get and stay organized. Make sure you have everything you need before you start to study.

3. Show up every time for class – both mentally and physically. By listening intently with focus, you can learn a lot of information the first time you hear it.

4. Take good notes during class, and read them over shortly after class. This will help you put new information into your brain in an organized manner, making it easier to recall it later. (Hint – Create pictures and diagrams both in your head and on paper while your are taking notes and listening.)

5. Turn off all devices that might distract you while studying. You may believe you are multi-tasking when you are doing your homework while watching TV or chatting online, but you are actually short circuiting your brain by continually starting and stopping. This can impede deep thinking and learning.

6. Remember – the more work you can get done at school, the less you'll have to do at home, so manage your time wisely.

7. Avoid cramming…it hurts your brain. Instead, make a study plan before a test and follow it.

8. Break big concepts up into smaller ones so you can understand them easier.

9. Use colored markers/pencils to highlight and categorize information. Everything is more **FUN** with color!

10. Create study games both with yourself and with others using flashcards, timers, acronyms, etc.

11. Ask for help when you need it!

12. Keep up with your homework – especially when you are absent. Homework allows you to practice and apply information, making it more retrievable. Chances are if it's in the homework, it's on the test.

13. Always read test questions carefully and don't spent too much time on any one question – move on and come back to it if you have time.

14. Make sure you get enough sleep so your brain isn't tired.

15. Believe in yourself! You'll be amazed at the difference attitude can make when you are trying to retrieve information from your brain!

As Will Foley once said:

"If you put a small price on your head…don't expect the rest of the world to raise it!"